# Uzuri, why did you do that?!

# Uzuri, why did you do that?!

*Written and illustrated by*
Uzuri Swift

Copyright © 2020 Uzuri Swift

ISBN: 9798570870390

PublishNation
www.publishnation.co.uk

*Dedicated to the best Mummy and Daddy*
*I could ask for. I love you!*

Once upon a time in a small town, in a small house lived Mummy, Daddy, and a sweet little girl called Uzuri.

"Goodbye Daddy!" said Uzuri, and off Daddy went to work.

Drip drip drip! Pitter patter!

"Look, Mummy! It is raining! Can I go play in the puddles?!" shouted out Uzuri, her face pressed against the window.

"OK, but first brush your–"

But we might never know what Mummy wanted Uzuri to brush, because Uzuri was already outside, in her pyjamas, barefoot, jumping around in the puddles.

Mummy yelped in horror and called Uzuri inside.

"Uzuri, why did you do that?!" cried out Mummy.

# Uzuri, why did you do that?!

"Before you step on the carpet, please wipe your–"

But we might never know what Mummy wanted Uzuri to first wipe, because Uzuri was already running around the room, splashing mud and water and goodness-knows-what everywhere.

Mummy yelped in horror and shouted for Uzuri to stop.

"Uzuri, why did you do that?!" cried out Mummy.

# Uzuri, why did you do that?!

"Stop! Please! Go to the bathroom and clean yourself up, and please remember to turn off the—"

But we might never know what Mummy wanted Uzuri to remember to turn off, because Uzuri had already shut the door.

Scrubba scrubba! Drip drip!

Ten minutes later, Uzuri bounded out of the bathroom, sparkling clean and nicely dressed in a blue jumper and blue trousers.

Mummy sighed with relief and went to see if Uzuri has turned off the tap.

Mummy looked inside the bathroom and yelped in horror.
Toothpaste was on the walls, the bath, and the sink.
Soap bubbles were everywhere, even in the toilet!
Mummy turned to face Uzuri, but Uzuri was gone.

"Uzuri, why did you do that?!" cried out Mum.

# Uzuri, why did you do that?!

"I am going to make myself breakfast now!" Uzuri called from the kitchen.

"Yes, you do that! But please remember to close the–"

But we might never know what Mummy wanted Uzuri to remember to close, because Uzuri had already made her breakfast!

"Well, that was quick," Mummy remarked and went to see if Uzuri had closed the fridge.

Mummy looked inside the kitchen and yelped in horror.

Butter, jam, marmite, and something suspiciously green were smeared on the walls, countertop, and the floor. The toaster looked destroyed, and the microwave was spewing out black smoke.

"Uzuri, why did you do that?!" cried out Mummy.

"What did you even make?" Mum asked wearily.

"I made a grilled cheese sandwich!" called Uzuri from the dining room.

Mummy sighed, put her hand to her head and went to join Uzuri.

"I will play in my room now!" Uzuri announced.

"Yes, play in your room, but could you please play–"

But we might never know how Mummy wanted Uzuri to play, because Uzuri had already gone upstairs.

The house was silent for a while.

"Aaah, peace at last!" sighed Mummy and picked up a book.

An hour later Uzuri bounded into the living room, beaming from ear to ear.

"Hello! I'm back!" she cried. "Come see what I've made!"

Mummy got up and followed Uzuri upstairs to her room.

Mummy peeped inside and yelped in horror.

Lego was scattered everywhere, play-doh was smeared on the walls, toys covered the floor, and Uzuri's bed was a crumpled heap of stuffed toys and duvet.

"Uzuri, why did you do that?!" cried out Mummy.

# Uzuri, why did you do that?!

"Yes, you have made something. A big mess! Clean this room this instant!"

Uzuri looked up at Mummy with big, pleading puppy eyes.

"Ok, I'll clean it all up," sighed Mummy. Who could say no to that face? "But please. No. More. Mess!"

"Why, I wouldn't dream of it!" smiled Uzuri and skipped off to the living room.

Mummy shook her head. "She's bound to make a mess!" she said to herself and got to work.

A few hours later, Mummy had completed her mission and went downstairs to the living room, bracing herself for the mess to come. She peered in. There was no yelp of horror. There was no big mess.

There was just Uzuri, standing next to a HUGE ROCKET!

"UZURI, **HOW** DID YOU DO **THAT**?!"

# Uzuri, **HOW** did you do **that**?!

## About the Author

Hi! My name is Uzuri Swift, and I love reading, writing, and any type of art. The story "Uzuri, why did you do that?!" I created a long time ago, and I have told it to my family many times! My family enjoyed the story very much (also drove my Mummy a little crazy) and I hope you enjoy it, too!

Printed in Great Britain
by Amazon

52080143R00015